For Sally and Lisa
H.M.

Text copyright © 1995 by Heather Maisner
Illustrations copyright © 1995 by Alan Baron

First U.S. edition 1995

Library of Congress Cataloging-in-Publication Data

Maisner, Heather.
The magic globe / Heather Maisner ; illustrated by Alan Baron.—1st U.S. ed.
ISBN 1-56402-445-8
1. Geographical recreations—Juvenile literature.   2. Picture puzzles—Juvenile literature.
[1. Geographical recreations.   2. Picture puzzles.]   I. Baron, Alan, 1942– ill.   II. Title.
GV1485.M35   1995
793.73—dc20   94-15164

2 4 6 8 10 9 7 5 3 1

Printed in Italy

The pictures in this book were done in line and watercolor.

Candlewick Press
2067 Massachusetts Avenue
Cambridge, Massachusetts 02140

THE MAGIC GLOBE

AN AROUND-THE-WORLD ADVENTURE GAME

HEATHER MAISNER   illustrated by ALAN BARON

CANDLEWICK PRESS
CAMBRIDGE, MASSACHUSETTS

CANADA AND ALASKA
pages 24 & 25
green

UNITED STATES
OF AMERICA
pages 14 & 15
green and blue

SOUTH AMERICA
pages 20 & 21
red

yellow

Great Uncle Atlas, a famous travel writer, has sent you a **yellow MAGIC GLOBE** and some instructions.

The globe was given to him by a traveler in the Andes Mountains. When you touch it and say the magic word, it sets off on a journey around the world, changes color, and hides. You too are sent on a journey.

Your task is to search for the globe and follow it back to **THIS PAGE**. But, before you start, read these instructions **VERY CAREFULLY** or you could be left in a faraway place.

INSTRUCTIONS

1. Touch the yellow globe and say "Zoomafar." When you turn the page, your journey will begin with a choice of two **AMAZING ADVENTURES.**

2. Choose either Amazing Adventure 1 or Amazing Adventure 2. The city where you begin will have an **orange** sign. Follow **THE ROUTE** to find the globe, which has changed color and is hiding close to the final clue.

Here are two examples:

3. Find the globe, memorize its color, and turn to the **WORLD MAP** above. Match the color to a globe on the map. This tells you which place to go to next.

4. Turn to this place, choose an Amazing Adventure, and follow **THE ROUTE**. Each time you find the globe, return to the map. If you are sent to the same place more than once, choose the other route.

5. Keep going until the globe becomes **yellow** again and leads you back to **THIS PAGE**.

SCANDINAVIA
pages 26 & 27

yellow and orange

EUROPE
pages 22 & 23

orange

RUSSIA AND NEIGHBORS
pages 28 & 29

red and yellow

CHINA, INDIA, AND NEIGHBORS
pages 8 & 9

yellow and green

JAPAN AND
NEIGHBORS
pages 16 & 17

blue

NORTHERN AFRICA,
THE MIDDLE EAST, AND NEIGHBORS

pages 18 & 19

red and blue

SOUTHERN
AND
CENTRAL
AFRICA
pages 12 & 13

orange and
yellow

N
NW NE
W E
SW SE
S

AUSTRALIA
AND
NEW ZEALAND
pages 10 & 11

blue and green

6. Play with the globe as often as you like. Each game will take you on a different journey—some short, some long. You may even find a way that takes you through every route!

One more thing. Each time Great Uncle Atlas travels, he loses some of his belongings. Please be on the lookout for them and bring them back with you. There are 22 items.

Have fun. Don't get lost. And look for Great Uncle Atlas too! You'll find him four times.

~ LOST ITEMS ~

pencil, flashlight, paintbrush, magnifying glass, calculator, key, yellow pencil, watch, scissors, paper clip, knapsack, glasses, ruler, green pencil, notepad, umbrella, tape, bottle of ink, camera, fountain pen, penknife, envelope

You have arrived in MADRAS **on the east coast of India. This vast land has many different languages and religions.**

~ THE ROUTE ~

☞ Go by rail NE to the crowded city of **CALCUTTA**.

☞ Follow the road NE over the sacred **RIVER GANGES** to **DHAKA**, capital of Bangladesh. Continue N to **MOUNT EVEREST**, the highest mountain in the world at 29,021 ft. The *yeti*—abominable snowman—is said to live here.

☞ Follow the road E to **LHASA**, capital of Tibet. Then go by road N through the mountains and E all the way to **LANZHOU** on the **YELLOW RIVER** in China. This is often called the world's muddiest river.

☞ Go NW by train beside the Great Wall and on to the oasis town of **TURPAN**. The Great Wall was begun 2,000 years ago to protect China from invaders from the north. It stretches over 3,510 miles.

☞ Go W, around the **TAKLAMAKAN DESERT**, to **KASHGAR**. Do not wander into the desert. Its name means: "If you go in, you'll never come out."

☞ Journey S through the spectacular mountains that separate China from Pakistan, to **ISLAMABAD**, capital of Pakistan.

☞ Continue S by road to **LAHORE**. Then take the train SE over the border to **NEW DELHI**, capital of India. Indian trains are very crowded; you may have to ride on the roof!

☞ SEEK THE MAGIC GLOBE
  Now it is orange and yellow.

You have arrived in HARBIN **in northeast China. More people live here than in any other country. More than one billion people in the world are Chinese.**

∼ THE ROUTE ∼

☞ Go SW by car past **SHENYANG** to **BEIJING**, China's capital. Visit the Forbidden City where the imperial family lived. For 500 years no ordinary person could enter here.

☞ Take the train S to **JINAN**. Then follow the **YELLOW RIVER** W to **ZHENGZHOU** and go on to **XI'AN**, once the capital of China. Visit life-size models of 8,000 soldiers buried more than 2,000 years ago.

☞ Go by road SW past **CHENGDU**, through the region where giant pandas live, to **LESHAN**. Can you see that huge figure? It's the largest statue of Buddha in the world and stands more than 230 ft high.

☞ Continue along the road S past **KUNMING** to **HANOI**, capital of Vietnam. Then go to **BANGKOK**, to the SW. You are now in the capital of Thailand.

☞ Sail S by ship to **SINGAPORE**, a small island but a major port, where it is hot and humid all year round.

☞ Sail NE across the **SOUTH CHINA SEA** all the way to **MANILA**. You are in the capital of the Philippines, which includes more than 7,000 islands.

☞ Now go by ship NW to **HONG KONG**. Its name means "fragrant harbor" and it is one of the most densely populated places on earth.

☞ SEEK THE MAGIC GLOBE
Now it is blue and green.

You have arrived in ALBANY **in the southwest of Australia, a country with desert in the center and tropical rain forest in the north. This country is sometimes called Oz for short.**

∼ THE ROUTE ∼

☞ Go by coach N to **PERTH**, where the sun shines an average of eight hours every day. Go swimming and sailing in the ocean.

☞ Fly E to the gold-mining town of **KALGOORLIE**. Take an elevator down under the ground to explore a gold mine.

☞ Travel by road all the way to **ADELAIDE**, to the SE. Visit the nearby Investigator Science Museum — hands-on fun for everyone. Then have a "barbie" — barbecue — on the beach.

☞ Take the train NW to **ALICE SPRINGS,** where the land is completely parched. Explore the desert landscape by camel.

☞ Journey SW to **AYERS ROCK**, the world's largest *monolith* — single block of stone. This is a sacred place to Aboriginal people, Australia's earliest inhabitants, who call it *Uluru*.

☞ Return to **ALICE SPRINGS**, then ride N in a jeep past **TENNANT CREEK** to **DARWIN**. Hot and sticky? Take a boat ride through the vast wetlands but watch out for crocodiles! See ancient Aboriginal rock art.

☞ Go by bus to the old pearling port of **BROOME**, to the southwest. Visit the nearby dinosaur footprint, said to be 130 million years old.

☞ **SEEK THE MAGIC GLOBE**
  Now it is orange and yellow.

You have arrived in BLUFF at the southern end of New Zealand. The Maoris—the first people to live here—called this mountainous country the "land of the long white cloud."

~THE ROUTE~

☞ Follow the road NE past **DUNEDIN** to **CHRISTCHURCH**. Pass sheep stations on the way. New Zealand has more sheep than people. There are at least 20 sheep to each person.

☞ Take the boat NE to **WELLINGTON**, capital of New Zealand. Hold on to your hat! In this city, known as "Windy Wellington," winds can blow up to 62 miles an hour.

☞ Go by car N to **ROTORUA**. Tired? Visit the hot springs and have a mud bath; see geysers more than 18 ft high. Then go N to **AUCKLAND**, the largest city in New Zealand.

☞ Cruise NW by boat across the sea to **SYDNEY** in Australia. Do you see that building in the shape of sails? It's the famous Sydney Opera House.

☞ Travel by train N past **PORT MACQUARIE** and **COFFS HARBOUR** to **BRISBANE**. Visit the nearby koala sanctuary and see animals found only in Australia.

☞ Go W by car past **TOOWOOMBA** to **CHARLEVILLE** and NW to **WINTON**. Do you see that large statue? It's Banjo Paterson, the poet and songwriter who wrote "Waltzing Matilda."

☞ Now go N to **CAIRNS** where it's hot all year round. Visit the Great Barrier Reef, the largest coral reef in the world, and see exotic underwater creatures.

☞ **SEEK THE MAGIC GLOBE**
Now it is green and blue.

You have arrived in MOGADISHU, **capital of Somalia on the northeast coast of Africa. Africa is where people say mankind began.**

~ THE ROUTE ~

☞ Sail SW along the coast to MOMBASA. Then go NW by train to NAIROBI. This is the capital of Kenya.

☞ Follow the road S to MT. KILIMANJARO and climb to the top of the snowcapped summit. You are now at the highest point in Africa.

☞ Take a hot air balloon NW past herds of wildebeest and zebra to LAKE VICTORIA. Fly on to KAMPALA, capital of Uganda.

☞ Go by road across the border to KISANGANI in Zaire. You are now in Zaire. Visit pygmies in the nearby rain forest. They are all less than 5 ft tall.

☞ Feeling hot? Take a river boat along the RIVER ZAIRE to LISALA in the northwest. This river used to be called the Congo.

☞ Go by road NW across the OUBANGUI RIVER to BANGUI, capital of the Central African Republic.

☞ Continue NW by bus to BOUAR. Do you see those huge standing stones? They were put up by an ancient civilization thousands of years ago.

☞ Go SW by bus past YAOUNDÉ to LAMBARÉNÉ in Gabon. Want to see some elephants? Few people live here, so the forests are full of wildlife.

☞ Continue SE by car to BRAZZAVILLE, capital of the Congo.

☞ SEEK THE MAGIC GLOBE

Now it is blue.

12

You have arrived in

SWAKOPMUND on the southwest coast of Africa in Namibia. **This country is mostly desert with some of the world's highest sand dunes—up to 100 ft high.**

~ THE ROUTE ~

☞ Take the train E to **WINDHOEK.** Then follow the road E through the **KALAHARI DESERT** to **MAUN** in Botswana. Pass Bushmen on the way. They are among the earliest-known inhabitants of southern Africa.

☞ Continue E over the border to the ruins of **GREAT ZIMBABWE.** This was a huge city about 600 years ago.

☞ Go by road past **BULAWAYO** to **VICTORIA FALLS** to the northwest. This waterfall is known locally as "the smoke that thunders." Did you bring an umbrella? Spray can fly up to 1650 ft.

☞ Continue by road NE past zebras and elephants to **LILONGWE,** capital of Malawi. Hungry? Have a feast of bananas, guavas, and mangoes.

☞ Go E to the port of **PEMBA.** Stow away on a boat sailing SE to **MAHAJANGA** on the island of Madagascar. Beware of sharks on the way!

☞ Go S by car to **TOLIARA.** Visit a petrified forest and see fossilized trees. Then fly SW to **MAPUTO,** capital of Mozambique.

☞ Take the train into South Africa past **JOHANNESBURG** to **KIMBERLEY** to the southwest. See that big hole? It's the world's biggest man-made hole and was dug for diamonds.

☞ **SEEK THE MAGIC GLOBE**
Now it is green and blue.

You have arrived in SEATTLE on the northwest coast of the United States of America. This huge country stretches from the Pacific Ocean in the west to the Atlantic Ocean in the east. It also includes Alaska and Hawaii.

~ THE ROUTE ~

☞ Sail S through the Pacific Ocean to **SAN FRANCISCO**. This city, built on forty hills, grew as a result of the gold rush in 1849.

☞ Go by car SE to **LOS ANGELES**. See Hollywood, home of the movies, and then go on to nearby **ANAHEIM** and visit Disneyland.

☞ Fly NE by helicopter to the **GRAND CANYON**. Look down steep cliffs to the Colorado River snaking through the valley 1 mile below.

☞ Cycle S past **PHOENIX**, then along the Apache Trail—the Apache tribe's old route across the land—to **TUCSON**. See nearby giant cacti that can grow to 43 ft and live up to 200 years.

☞ Go by car E past **EL PASO** and **SAN ANTONIO** to **HOUSTON**. Visit the LBJ Space Center and see the mission control that landed the first man on the moon in 1969.

☞ Take the train NW to **OKLAHOMA CITY**. Pass large herds of cattle on the way. Go NW by plane to **DENVER**.

☞ Continue N to **MOUNT RUSHMORE**. Do you see those huge faces carved into the cliffs? They are portraits of four U.S. presidents.

☞ SEEK THE MAGIC GLOBE
Now it is blue.

You have arrived in **BOSTON** on the northeast coast of the United States of America, a country made up of fifty separate states. It was here that the War of Independence began in 1775.

～THE ROUTE～

☞ Take a Greyhound bus SW to **NEW YORK CITY** and visit the Statue of Liberty. Then go SW to **WASHINGTON D.C.**, capital of the United States and home of the U.S. government.

☞ Go by car NW to **DETROIT**, known as the Motor City. Visit the Henry Ford Museum. See early cars and the bicycle shop where the Wright brothers built the first plane.

☞ Continue W to **CHICAGO**. Take the elevator to the top of the Sears Tower and discover how the world looks from its tallest building.

☞ Catch a train NW to **MINNEAPOLIS**—its name means "city of water"—and you are now at the mighty **MISSISSIPPI RIVER**. Go by boat S to **ST. LOUIS**.

☞ Continue S by boat, past **MEMPHIS**, all the way to **NEW ORLEANS**, where jazz music began.

☞ Now fly SE across the **GULF OF MEXICO** to **MIAMI**. Then go N to **CAPE CANAVERAL**. Just look at that rocket! This is the Kennedy Space Center, where manned space flights are launched.

☞ Take a train NW to **ATLANTA**. Thirsty? Have a Coca-Cola. It was invented right here!

☞ **SEEK THE MAGIC GLOBE**

Now it is red.

You have arrived in FUKUOKA in southwest Japan on Kyushu, one of the four major islands of Japan, a country with more than 3,900 islands.

~ THE ROUTE ~

☞ Go by road S to **KAGOSHIMA**. Did you bring an umbrella? Ash from a nearby live volcano often falls on the city. Cycle through subtropical scenery to **MIYAZAKI** in the east.

☞ Like to try a mud bath? Go N to **BEPPU** where underground volcanic activity has created hot springs. Bring an egg and watch it boil in a bubbling mud pool.

☞ Go E by ferry to **MATSUYAMA** on the island of Shikoku. Feeling hungry? Japan is a fishing nation and a favorite dish is *sashimi*—raw seafood.

☞ Go E along the road toward **TAKAMATSU**, then N across the bridge that links Shikoku to the main island, called Honshu.

☞ Cycle E past **HIMEJI** to **KYOTO**, the ancient capital of Japan. Visit temples and Zen gardens of gravel and rock.

☞ Go S to the port of **OSAKA**. Sail SW past the islands of **SHIKOKU** and **KYUSHU**. Now sail to the port of **PUSAN**. You are now in South Korea, sometimes known as "land of the morning calm" because the countryside is so peaceful.

☞ Take the train NW to the capital, **SEOUL**. Visit the royal Secret Garden. See pavilions, ponds, and a 400-year-old plum tree.

☞ Continue NW to **PYONGYANG**, capital of North Korea.

☞ **SEEK THE MAGIC GLOBE**

Now it is red.

You have arrived in SAPPORO on Hokkaido, the major island in northern Japan. In winter the temperature often falls to –30°F.

~ THE ROUTE ~

☞ Catch a bus NE to **DAISETSUZAN** Nature Park and hike through the mountains. Japan's largest wild animal, the brown bear, lives here.

☞ Go SE to **KUSHIRO** and on to **HAKODATE** in the southwest. Take a train under the **TSUGARU STRAIT** to **AOMORI** through the world's longest undersea tunnel— 33.5 miles.

☞ Continue S to **MORIOKA**. Then travel at 150 miles per hour on the bullet train to **FUKUSHIMA**. You are in the main rice-growing area, and a Japanese word for rice—*gohan*—also means meal.

☞ Continue by train to **TOKYO**, capital of Japan. Visit shops selling the world's latest electronic equipment.

☞ Go by road SW to **MT. FUJI**, Japan's highest mountain. This dormant volcano is often called "mountain where the gods dwell."

☞ Continue west to **NAGOYA**. Like to know how the *samurai* lived? Travel NE to **MATSUMOTO** and explore the six-story black castle, known as Crow Castle.

☞ Go NE by car to **NIIGATA**. You are now in one of the heaviest snowfall regions in the world, where the winds blow across from Siberia in Russia.

☞ Sail NW by ship across the **SEA OF JAPAN** to **VLADIVOSTOK** in Russia. This is the last stop on the Trans-Siberian railway, which runs all the way from Moscow.

☞ SEEK THE MAGIC GLOBE

Now it is green.

You have arrived in ALGIERS, capital of Algeria, on the northern coast of Africa. Africa includes more than fifty countries.

~ THE ROUTE ~

☞ Go by road W to **TANGIER** in Morocco. Thirsty? Visit the narrow streets of the *medina*—old city—and stop for a glass of mint tea.

☞ Catch a train to **MARRAKESH** in the southwest. Explore the winding alleys of the famous *souk*—market.

☞ Make your way E across the snowcapped **ATLAS MOUNTAINS** to **BENI ABBÈS** in Algeria. You are now in the Sahara Desert, the largest desert in the world.

☞ Continue to **TAMANRASSET** in the southeast. Can you see blue-robed *Tuaregs* with goats? They are nomads who move from place to place in search of grazing land.

☞ Fill your flask with water and ride SW by camel to **TIMBUKTU** in Mali. This was once the center of the gold trade in West Africa.

☞ Hot and tired? You're in luck. It's the wet season and the **NIGER RIVER** is high. Paddle in a dugout canoe SW past **DJENNÉ** to **BAMAKO**. Avoid the hippos as you go!

☞ Ride SE on a truck through the Ivory Coast to **ABIDJAN**. Go swimming in the ocean.

☞ Now catch a boat going W around the bulge of Africa to **FREETOWN**, capital of Sierra Leone. This means "lion mountains."

☞ SEEK THE MAGIC GLOBE
Now it is blue and green.

You have arrived in KABUL, capital of Afghanistan, in the northeast. Afghanistan is a landlocked country with great mountains, burning deserts, valleys, and plains.

~ THE ROUTE ~

☞ Fly SW across the **MARGO DESERT**—or "Desert of Death"—to **MUSCAT**, capital of Oman, in the Middle East. On the way, see camels. Now take a ferry NW to **BANDAR ABBAS** in Iran.

☞ Go by bus NW to **SHIRAZ**. Visit palaces built more than 2,500 years ago.

☞ Continue by bus NW past the city of **ESFAHAN** and across the border to **BAGHDAD**, the capital of Iraq. You are now in the region known in ancient times as Mesopotamia.

☞ Go by car SW to **AMMAN**, capital of Jordan. Continue NW to **JERUSALEM**, capital of Israel. Visit holy sites of three religions: Judaism, Islam, and Christianity.

☞ Take a bus SW across the **SINAI DESERT** to the **SUEZ CANAL**. This shipping canal links the Mediterranean Sea, in the north, with the Red Sea.

☞ Continue W to **CAIRO**, capital of Egypt. Then sail S in a *felucca*—river boat—along the **RIVER NILE**, the longest river in the world, to **LUXOR** to the southeast. Many pharaohs were buried nearby in the Valley of the Kings.

☞ Follow the river S past **WADI HALFA** to **KHARTOUM**, capital of Sudan.

☞ SEEK THE MAGIC GLOBE

Now it is yellow.

You have arrived in RIO DE JANEIRO, **halfway down the east coast of Brazil. This is the largest country in South America and the only one where Portuguese is the national language. Most speak Spanish.**

~ THE ROUTE ~

☞ Go N by bus to **SALVADOR**. See boys practicing *capoeira*—a form of martial arts and dance, performed to the rhythm of local music. Continue NE to **RECIFE**.

☞ Go by bus to **BELÉM** to the northwest. Then sail W along the **AMAZON RIVER** to **MANAUS**. Listen to the sounds of the wildlife. You are traveling through the world's largest rain forest.

☞ Fly NW past the **ANGEL FALLS** to **CARACAS**, capital of Venezuela. This waterfall, the highest in the world, plunges 2,330 ft from a flat-topped mountain.

☞ Go S by bus past **BOGOTÁ**, capital of Colombia, and SW to **QUITO**, capital of Ecuador. Visit ancient stone statues at nearby **SAN AGUSTÍN**.

☞ Go S to **GUAYAQUIL**, then sail W to the **GALÁPAGOS ISLANDS**. Look out for giant tortoises and other creatures unique to these islands.

☞ Fly SE past **LIMA**, capital of Peru, and on to **NAZCA**. See those strange drawings in the desert? They were made 2,000 years ago.

☞ Ride a donkey NE to **CUZCO**, once the capital of the Inca Empire, which stretched from Colombia in the north to Chile in the south. Visit Inca ruins.

☞ SEEK THE MAGIC GLOBE
  Now it is green.

S O U T H   A T L A N T I C   O C E A N

SOUTH GEORGIA

N
NW · NE
W · E
SW · SE
S

PORTO ALEGRE

URUGUAY

MONTEVIDEO

BUENOS AIRES

MAR DEL PLATA

PARAGUAY

BAHÍA BLANCA

ARGENTINA

CONCORDIA

CÓRDOBA

ROSARIO

COLORADO

TRELEW

COMODORO RIVADAVIA

FALKLAND ISLANDS

STANLEY

RIO GALLEGOS

SAN JUAN

ANDES MOUNTAINS

BARILOCHE

PUNTA ARENAS

USHUAIA

TIERRA DEL FUEGO

ATACAMA DESERT

SANTIAGO

CONCEPCIÓN

PUERTO MONTT

CHILE

You have arrived in USHUAIA at the very south of Argentina. Here on the island of Tierra del Fuego—"Land of Fire"—you are as far south as you can go before Antarctica.

☞ **THE ROUTE** ☜

☞ Fly N to **TRELEW**. You are crossing the flat region known as Patagonia, which comes from a Spanish word for big feet.

☞ Journey by bus NW to **BARILOCHE**. Go skiing or hiking in the Andes Mountains.

☞ Take the train NE across the *pampas*—grassy plains—to **BAHIÁ BLANCA** and then N to **BUENOS AIRES**, Argentina's capital.

☞ Go by car NE to **PORTO ALEGRE**. See *gauchos*—cowboys—on horseback. They look after large herds of cattle.

☞ Fly N to **ASUNCIÓN**, capital of Paraguay. Ride on a truck NW over scrubland to **POTOSÍ** in Bolivia, one of the highest cities in the world at 13,350 ft.

☞ Go by train SW to **ANTOFAGASTA**. You are crossing the **ATACAMA DESERT**, the driest desert in the world. Parts of this desert have never seen rain or many living plants or animals.

☞ Continue S by train to **SANTIAGO**, capital of Chile. This long, thin country lies between the Pacific Ocean and the Andes Mountains, which stretch the whole length of South America.

☞ **SEEK THE MAGIC GLOBE**
Now it is yellow and orange.

You have arrived in LISBON, capital of Portugal in southwestern Europe. Europe has more than thirty countries.

~ THE ROUTE ~

☞ Go by car NE to **MADRID**, capital of Spain. Then go E past **ZARAGOZA** to **BARCELONA** on the Mediterranean Sea. Hungry? Try *paella*—a rice dish with meat and seafood.

☞ Go by bus NE past the **PYRENEES**, the mountains that separate Spain from France, to **NÎMES**. Continue SE to the port of **MARSEILLE**.

☞ Go N by road past **LYON**, once the capital of *Gaul*—ancient France—to **STRASBOURG**, home of the European parliament.

☞ Sail along the **RIVER RHINE** past **BONN** to **COLOGNE** in the N. Go carefully! A maiden called the Lorelei is said to sit on a rock and lure sailors to their death with her singing.

☞ Cycle NW to **AMSTERDAM**, capital of the Netherlands. Then go by bus SW past **BRUSSELS**, the capital of Belgium, to **PARIS**, capital of France. Climb the Eiffel Tower.

☞ Fly NW all the way to **DUBLIN**, capital of the Republic of Ireland. This city was founded by the Vikings.

☞ Take the ferry E to **HOLYHEAD** in Wales. Then go by bus SE to **LONDON**, capital of the United Kingdom. Do you see that clock tower? It's called Big Ben.

☞ Now go by train NW to **EDINBURGH**, the capital of Scotland. Visit the castle. Then go to the Museum of Childhood.

☞ **SEEK THE MAGIC GLOBE**
Now it is red and blue.

You have arrived in ROME, **capital of Italy, the country in the shape of a boot in the Mediterranean Sea.**

~ THE ROUTE ~

☞ Go NW by bus to **PISA**. Can you see that leaning tower? It's the bell tower of Pisa's cathedral, built in the twelfth century.

☞ Continue NE to **VENICE** where there are canals instead of streets. Tour the city by waterbus.

☞ Follow the road N over the Alps, which form Italy's northern border, to **MUNICH** in Germany.

☞ Take the train N to **BERLIN**, capital of Germany. See the remains of the Berlin Wall, which divided the city for 30 years until 1990.

☞ Follow the **RIVER ODER** SE to **WROCLAW** in Poland. Then take the road SW to **PRAGUE**. You are now in the capital of the Czech Republic.

☞ Go by car SE to **BUDAPEST**, capital of Hungary, on the **RIVER DANUBE**. Feeling hungry? Try apple strudel—light, thin pastry filled with apples, raisins, and nuts.

☞ Sail down the **DANUBE** to **BELGRADE** in the southeast. This river flows through eight countries.

☞ Do you dare visit Dracula's castle? Go E to **TIRGOVISTE** where the real Count Dracula lived. Then go on to **BUCHAREST**, capital of Romania.

☞ Now fly SW to **ATHENS**, capital of Greece. Visit the ruins of the Acropolis, built 2,500 years ago.

☞ SEEK THE MAGIC GLOBE

Now it is yellow and green.

You have arrived in NOME on the west coast of Alaska. This vast wilderness is the largest state in the United States of America.

~ THE ROUTE ~

☞ It's Sunday. Fly SW past **GAMBELL** on **ST. LAWRENCE ISLAND** and across the International Date Line. This imaginary line marks the place where each new day begins. Here it is Monday! Turn back and fly E to **ALAKANUK** where it is still Sunday.

☞ Paddle NE in a *kayak*—small canoe—up the **YUKON RIVER** to **TANANA**. Continue on to **FAIRBANKS**. Take the train S past **MT. McKINLEY**, the highest mountain in North America, to **ANCHORAGE**.

☞ Go by road NE to **DAWSON** in Canada. This was once a booming gold-mining town, the center of the Klondike gold rush 100 years ago.

☞ Catch a plane and fly E to **YELLOWKNIFE**. Look down on mountains, home to moose and grizzly bears. Go fishing when you arrive.

☞ Sail SW across **GREAT SLAVE LAKE** to **HAY RIVER**. Take the train to **EDMONTON** to the southeast. Then continue S to **CALGARY**. Interested in dinosaurs? Visit the nearby dinosaur park.

☞ Go by bus W past **BANFF** to **VANCOUVER**. Do you see those totem poles? They were made by native tribes such as the Haida, who have lived here for thousands of years.

☞ SEEK THE MAGIC GLOBE

Now it is red and yellow.

You have arrived in ST. JOHN'S **on** NEWFOUNDLAND ISLAND **in southeastern Canada. Many parts of this huge country are uninhabited.**

☞ Take a boat W to **GASPÉ** at the start of the **ST. LAWRENCE RIVER**, the world's longest canal system.

☞ Go SW by boat past **MONTREAL** in French-speaking Canada as far as **NIAGARA FALLS** in English-speaking Canada.

☞ Sail across the **GREAT LAKES** NW to **THUNDER BAY**. These lakes form part of the border between Canada and the United States.

☞ Take a bus W past **WINNIPEG** to **REGINA**. Do you see those men on horseback? They are known as Mounties—Royal Canadian Mounted Police.

☞ Go N by car past **SASKATOON** to **PRINCE ALBERT**. See moose on the way. You are in "big sky country" now, where wheat grows across vast prairie lands.

☞ Catch the train NE to **CHURCHILL**. Tour the flat, frozen land and see polar bears.

☞ Fly in a ski plane NE over **HUDSON BAY** to **IQALUIT** on **BAFFIN ISLAND**. Look down on beluga whales.

☞ Go NW by snowmobile to **CAPE DORSET**. Visit an Inuit—Eskimo—family. Inuit means "people" in their language.

☞ SEEK THE MAGIC GLOBE
Now it is yellow and orange.

You have arrived in REYKJAVÍK, capital of Iceland, in the northwest. This rugged island is one of the most active volcanic areas on earth and has many hot springs and mud pools.

THE ROUTE

☞ Fly to BODØ on the NW coast of Norway. Look down at the whales. Take the coastal steamer NE past TROMSØ to NORTH CAPE.

☞ Continue by steamer to KIRKENES in the southeast, near the Russian border. You are in the land of the midnight sun where for parts of the summer the sun never sets and in the winter it seldom rises.

☞ Find your way by husky dog and sled SW to KARASJOK. Do you see those people herding reindeer? They are Sami, or Lapps, who have lived here in Europe's last wilderness since ancient times. Continue SW to KAUTOKEINO.

☞ Go by bus SE all the way to ROVANIEMI. Visit the Santa Claus Workshop Village. Letters are sent here to Santa from children all over the world.

☞ Fly W by ski plane over the border as far as ARJEPLOG in Sweden. You are now beside the deepest of Sweden's many lakes. One of these lakes is said to have a monster!

☞ SEEK THE MAGIC GLOBE

Now it is orange.

You have arrived in COPENHAGEN, capital of Denmark, in the south of Scandinavia. Denmark includes over 400 islands.

☞ Are you a Lego fan? Fly W to **BILLUND** and visit Legoland. It's made of more than 30 million Lego bricks.

☞ Fly N to **OSLO**, capital of Norway, and visit the Viking Ship Museum.

☞ Take the train W to **BERGEN**. Then go by boat along the coast past **ÅLESUND** to **TRONDHEIM** in the northeast. On the way explore the *fjords*—deep fingers of sea reaching between steep mountains.

☞ Take the bus SE to **FALUN** in Sweden. Look down into the giant copper pit, 325 ft deep and 1,300 ft across.

☞ Go SW by road to **ÖREBRO** and visit the medieval castle. Then go E to **STOCKHOLM**, Sweden's capital.

☞ Go NE by ferry to **TURKU**, the oldest town in Finland. Then cycle SE to **HELSINKI**, Finland's capital. You are on the King's Road, the old route that links Norway, Sweden, and Finland with St. Petersburg in Russia.

☞ Now take a bus NE to **SAVONLINNA**. Go fishing, canoeing, and rowing on the lakes. Finland has 198,000 lakes.

☞ **SEEK THE MAGIC GLOBE**
Now it is red and yellow.

You have arrived in MURMANSK, **a major port in northwestern Russia, the largest country in the world. It stretches for more than 5,580 miles from west to east.**

~ THE ROUTE ~

☞ Go S by train to ST. PETERSBURG. Do you see that statue of a man on horseback? It's Peter the Great, who built this city on marshy swampland and made it Russia's capital.

☞ Go by road SE to MOSCOW, now the capital of Russia. Travel around the city by metro and see magnificent underground stations decorated with chandeliers and statues. Then go to the ballet.

☞ Continue by car past BRYANSK to KIEV, capital of the Ukraine in the southwest. Go to the circus and see the clowns.

☞ Go by road S to ODESSA and cross the water to YALTA. You are now in the region known as the Crimea. Visit Fairy Tale Valley and see statues of characters from well-known fairy stories.

☞ Continue by boat SE across the BLACK SEA to Georgia and tour the capital, TBILISI. Go hiking in the mountains called the Caucasus, where many people live to be more than 100 years old.

☞ Follow the road SE to BAKU, capital of Azerbaijan. You are now beside the Caspian Sea, the largest lake in the world. Like to try some caviar? It is made from the tiny eggs of the large sturgeon fish that swim in the lake.

☞ SEEK THE MAGIC GLOBE

Now it is red and blue.

You have arrived in NORILSK in the northeast. You are in Siberia, the vast eastern region of Russia that continues for thousands of miles to the east from here.

~ THE ROUTE ~

☞ Take the road past **IGARKA** all the way to **KRASNOYARSK** to the south. You are traveling through the *taiga*—coniferous forest. This forest is the largest in the world. Brown bear, elk, and wolves live here.

☞ Go SW to **NOVOSIBIRSK** on the Trans-Siberian Railway, the longest railway in the world. Cold and hungry? Try Siberian *pelmeni*—minced meat in parcels of pasta, served with vinegar.

☞ Sail NW along the **RIVER OB** all the way to **SALEKHARD**. Tour the *tundra*—flat, treeless land—where people have lived for centuries raising reindeer.

☞ Take the road NW to **VORKUTA**. Then fly S over the **URAL MOUNTAINS** to **SEROV**. These mountains form the natural frontier between Europe in the west and Asia in the east.

☞ Take the road to **KURGAN** to the southeast. Then go S by bus across the *steppe*—flat grassy plain—to **KARAGANDA** in Kazakhstan.

☞ Interested in space travel? Go to **BAIKONUR SPACE CENTER** to the southwest. Yuri Gagarin, the first man in space, was launched from here in 1961.

☞ Go by train SE to **TASHKENT**, capital of Uzbekistan. Then travel W to **SAMARKAND**. You are on the ancient Silk Road, once the only link between China and the West.

☞ SEEK THE MAGIC GLOBE

Now it is orange.